# *Amanda's Book*

Design: Ruth Ohi

Annick Press Ltd.

Annick Press gratefully acknowledges
the support of The Canada Council and
the Ontario Arts Council

**Canadian Cataloguing in Publication Data**

Westell, Kerry
     Amanda's book

ISBN 1-55037-185-1 (bound)   ISBN 1-55037-182-7 (pbk.)

I. Ohi, Ruth.   II. Title.

PS8595.E884A78 1991       jC813′.54       C91-093472-X
PZ7.W488Am 1991

The art in this book was rendered
in water colour and ink.
The text has been set in Cheltenham
light by Attic Typesetting

Distribution for Canada and the USA:

Firefly Books Ltd.,
250 Sparks Avenue
North York, Ontario M2H 2S4

 ∞  Printed on acid-free paper.

Printed and bound in Canada
by Friesen Printers

# Amanda's Book

by Kerry Westell
Art by Ruth Ohi

Annick Press Ltd.
Toronto

My Mom gave me a scrapbook for my birthday.
It was a big book with wide pages and a red cover.
I found some pictures I liked in a magazine, and I
cut them out and put them in the scrapbook.

Then I cut out some chairs and a table. I put the whole dining room in my scrapbook. "The house seems smaller somehow," said my Mom.

I went outside and cut out the moon.
My Dad came home from jogging and asked,
"Where's the moon tonight? And isn't the house
smaller?"

The next day I cut out a cloud I liked and put it under the moon. Then I decided to cut out the whole sky and put it in too. It was pretty big, so I used two pages.

Birds took to walking around on the ground. People kept bumping into them. "This is not convenient," they said.

I cut out the sun. It got dark. Now everyone started to get lost. My Dad kept saying, "Where's the sun? Where's the moon? Where's the dining room? And what are all these birds doing on the ground?"

The cat saw sunlight coming out of the scrapbook and went in after it. "No, kitty!" I cried and followed him in.

It was all jumbled up inside. There were clouds under my feet and trees over my head.

I followed the cat past a page of bicycles.
We ran across the two pages of sky.

I finally caught up to him on the moon.

"Now kitty," I said, "how do we get back?"

"If you ask me," said the cat, "you'll hope the wind ruffles the pages of the book and blows us out of here. It should be along soon; it's practically the only thing you didn't cut out."

Sure enough, the wind came along in a little while, looking for the rest of the world. It ruffled the scrapbook open and everything blew out.

For a few days lots of things were out of place. There were umbrellas in the sky and clouds around people's knees. Not everybody had their own bicycles back either. But we sorted that stuff out.

Now that things have calmed down, I like to sit with my cat and watch the moon. We talk about the seasons, the oceans, and the stars, and about how much I enjoyed collecting them.

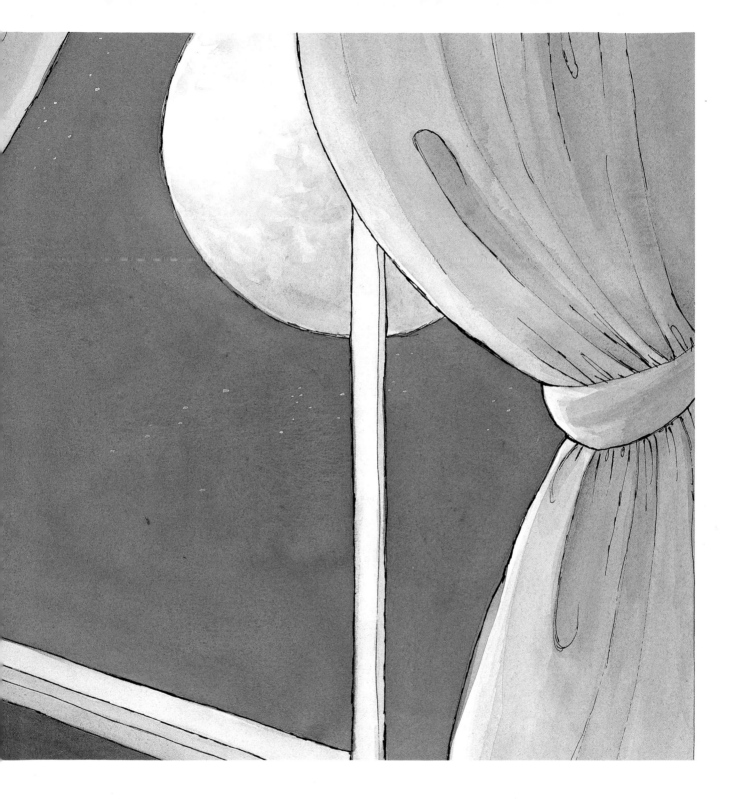

It was kind of fun putting things in a scrapbook,
so I've asked for a notebook for my next birthday,
and I'm writing *everything* in it!

My name is
Amanda Louise.
My Mom's name is
Mom and my Dad's name
Dad. My cat's name is
Richard. Don't call hi
Rick 'cause he hates it
He has a secret I
won't tell. One da
he was looking at a bir